T

AN AUTO-BIOGRAPHY

A delightful read! "T" has given children an opportunity to view America's past through the "eyes" and adventures of a wise-cracking, good-natured, endearing Model-T Ford. Feather Schwartz Foster's unique style has introduced us to a colorful cast of characters who remind us of those dear folks who graced our nation's "growing up years". Adults will reminisce while reading this with their children, and it will provide a great reading experience for the whole family. ~ *Colleen Fantini*

A modern fairy tale. Reading Feather's book actually brought tears to my eyes. Chalk it up to age, if you will, mine - but a truncated American memoir, traveling through the last eighty-five years, as seen through the headlights of a Model-T, is charming and inspiring in an old-fashioned way. Made me long for a return to innocence. ~ *Paul Guskin*

Cars have feelings, too! Feather Schwartz Foster offers bright, new perspectives to the familiar road trip, bringing that oft-ignored supporting character onto center stage. Children will delight at the adventures and misadventures of an old Model-T who finally has a chance to tell it like it was. ~ *Ken Goldberg, Ph.D., author of* **The Homework Trap**

"T" is a charming, adventurous, imaginative read that gently weaves in a bit of history. What a fun way to learn about America's early cars and lifestyle. Parents will find the saga of "T" equally engaging as they read aloud to their child or snuggle up to listen as their young reader recites the account. ~ *Brenda Nixon, Speaker, Writer, Educator and author of* **Parenting Power in the Early Years**

T
AN AUTO-BIOGRAPHY

by
Feather Schwartz Foster

Red Engine Press
Key West, FL

Published by **Red Engine Press**

Library of Congress Control Number: 2006935739

ISBN (10): 0-9785158-3-8
ISBN (13): 978-0-9785158-3-6

Illustrations and Cover by
Kathe Gogolewski

Printed in the United States of America

Red Engine Press
1107 Key Plaza #158
Key West, FL 33040

"T" An Auto-Biography

Chapter 1 - I GET BOUGHT

I am a Model-T Ford. You can call me "T" for short. This is my autobiography. Get that? An *AUTO*-biography! I've had a lot of adventures in my long life - lots of owners, lots of good times, and a few not-so-good times. But all in all, it's been a fine life.

It started in 1920. Maybe 1921. I forget. But it was a very long time ago. I rolled off Mister Henry Ford's assembly line bright-eyed and bushy-tailed and spanking-shiny new. I was jet black and polished to a high gloss. I had a running board and a spare tire, and real leather seats. Oh, I was a handsome fellow, just waiting for somebody to buy me and start me on a life of excitement. I was going places!

In those days, they didn't have fancy-dancy showrooms. They just put a small advertisement in some of the newspapers and magazines, and waited for people to come to them. And they did! They came by the hundreds! And by the thousands! Mister Henry Ford had perfected his horseless carriage so that most people could afford them, and automobiles were selling like hotcakes!

One fine day, a distinguished-looking gentleman came in response to an ad he had seen in the newspaper. His name was John H. Wilson, of Smallville. *Doctor* John H. Wilson. *Very* impressive. "Yessir, Dr. Wilson," the salesman said eagerly, "I have just the car for you! It's the latest technology from the Ford Motor Company." He led Dr. Wilson over to where I was, and continued. "This baby is equipped with everything! It can easily go twenty-five, maybe thirty miles an hour." Dr. Wilson looked at the salesman in amazement. "Twenty-five miles an hour?" he said incredulously. "That's a little fast for me. No sir, a nice, safe fifteen, twenty miles an hour is fast enough for anyone."

"Oh yes," agreed the salesman, as he began to show me off to my prospective new owner. "Just look! This buggy has soft cushioned seats for long rides." He opened the door and showed the Doctor my real leather seats. "And," the salesman continued, "This car has lights that you can turn on and off! That should be perfect for your, ha-

ha, night-time deliveries." The salesman liked to joke. He turned my headlights on and off, with just a flick of a switch. Doctor Wilson seemed impressed. I was on my very best Sunday behavior, because I had taken a liking to the doctor, and hoped he would buy me.

"And," the salesman said, squeezing a contraption on my dashboard, "this hot little item has a *horn*! Yup, a *horn* to alert oncoming traffic." I beeped my horn in my best baritone voice. "Oh, these babies are selling like hotcakes, Doc. Like *hotcakes*." The salesman beeped my horn some more. "And believe me," he continued, "there *will* be traffic."

Doc Wilson opened my door and slammed it shut. Then he walked around me very slowly and lifted my hood to inspect my engine. And then, for absolutely no reason at all, he kicked my tires. That hurt. I don't know why people kick tires, but everybody seems to like doing it. "Very nice," said the Doctor. "Ver-ry nice. You know, a small town doctor just can't get to emergencies fast enough in a horse and buggy. And I really should keep up with the latest innovations. Besides, my old horse is going lame."

"Well this buggy should last you a good long

time," said the salesman. "It's a deal!" said Doc Wilson. "Three hundred dollars! It's a lot of money, but I think it'll be worth it." He paid the salesman, shook his hand and I was off to my very first home.

Chapter 2 - SMALLVILLE

Doc Wilson lived in Smallville, a nice little town. T'weren't too many cars here. Still mostly here, mostly horses. I tried being friendly, but the horses didn't take to me much, - especially when Doc Wilson beeped my horn.

I was there as the town grew. They had a nice general store which also served as the post office. There was a small hotel and a school and a firehouse. And lots of houses and farms. I got to know my way around quickly, since Doc took me everywhere.

I was there when he set Mr. Bundy's leg. He broke it when he tried to pull out an old tree stump and tripped on the roots. And I was there when Mrs. McDivitt had her appendix operation. That was an experience! Doc usually sent people to the County Hospital for major surgery like that, but Mrs. McDivitt's appendix was an emergency, so Doc operated it out right on her kitchen table!

And I was there when the entire Robbins family came down with the measles. Mother, Father and five little Robbinses. All full of red spots. The neighbors were bringing food and leaving it on the doorstep since they didn't want to catch the measles.

And it seemed like every few days Doc Wilson was off delivering a baby. I don't know where he got 'em from, but he'd leave Mrs. Smith's house, and by golly, there was a baby. Then he'd go to Mrs. Jones' house, and *how-about-that*!!! Another baby! Town grew so much that they tore down the old school and put up a new one - all on account of the new babies Doc was delivering. They put down real roads, too, with tar, not dirt. That was because more and more cars were coming to town. I had company! And with more cars, I made a new friend. Fred Mahoney, the town's first automobile mechanic.

"Nothin' wrong with this old buggy that a few new spark plugs, an oil change and maybe a tune-up now 'n then won't cure," Fred told Doc, as he checked my engine. "Well, I try to keep old T in good shape," the Doctor replied. "I just don't know what I would do without a car these days,

Fred. The town's grown so fast! Why in just five years, the population has nearly doubled! We've got more than five hundred families now!"

"You should know, Doc," Fred said. "You delivered most of 'em." "I suppose so," Doc replied, as Fred slammed down my hood and finished adjusting my crank case. "How much do I owe you?" "It's on the house, Doc. Remember? I promised you free service for a year after you delivered Peggy." "That makes four now, doesn't it, Fred?" asked the Doc, trying to remember. "Yup," said the mechanic. "Fred Junior, Tim, Joe, and finally a daughter. Peggy. Hey," he said, changing the subject, "Speaking of kids, I hear your boy Jim will be going off to the university soon."

"That's right," said Doc. "Jim's going to study business. And you know, I'm thinking of getting a new car for myself."

I was thunderstruck! Doc getting a new car? What about me? What would I do? Where would I go? I liked Smallville. I liked living with Doc Wilson. I didn't want him to get a new car! No way!

"Yup," continued the Doc. "I think I'll get me a

Pierce Arrow. It's bigger. I'll let Jim take the Model-T to the University."

Chapter 3 - JIM

Well that was a different story. Jim Wilson was the best, best, *best* pal a Model-T could ever have. Doc was good to me, sure he was. But Jim *loved* me! And I loved Jim. He would wash and polish me and shine me up bright as new, so you could see your face in my fender. He'd make sure I was in tip-top, A-number-one condition. And I always had plenty of gasoline. I never went hungry.

"Well, T, ol' buddy," Jim would say to me because he always talked to me when we were alone, "We're off to college now! You 'n me. A team! You'll be all shiny, and won't *we* impress the ladies!" He tied a "State U" pennant on my hood, and off we went.

I mean to tell you, there's nothing like a college education to broaden your horizons! Jim was a smart boy, all right. He studied hard and got good grades. But Jim also liked to have fun, and boy-o-boy did we have fun. Jim was a baseball player on the varsity team. Shortstop. He was pretty good. I went to all the games. And I went to all the picnics and parties and dances. Yessiree, we definitely had fun.

But something new was about to happen in our life. Couldn't quite put my finger on it at first, but then, after a couple of months, all the pieces started falling into place. Yup. A *big* change was about to occur, and that change was called . . . ANNABEL.

I could tell from the start that Annabel was something special. For one thing, Jim and I were going to her house an awful lot. Jim even played a special tune on my horn just for Annabel. "Beep-beepa-beep-beep. Beep-beep." And Annabel always sat in the front seat.

One time Jim decided to teach Annabel how to drive. That was a memorable experience.

"Now Annabel," Jim said, "the first thing you do is crank 'im up." He handed Annabel my crank, and she tried to get me started. "No, no, honey," Jim said. "A little harder. Put some moxie into it." He took the crank and showed her how to do it. "Now you try," he said. Annabel took the crank, grinned at me and said, "C'mon, T, you can do it! I know you can." I liked it when she talked to me. She patted me gently on the hood, and then and there I knew why Jim and I liked this girl. I started right up.

"OK, Annabel, now quick! Jump in!" said Jim, as he and Annabel hopped in. "Now first thing you do is step on the clutch with your left foot. Down here," he pointed. "No, not that one . . . the other one." I lurched. "Here! Here, Annabel, with your *left* foot." I made a sharp move to the right.

"OK, honey. Now shift into gear . . ." "What's gear?" "It's this stick, Annabel," Jim said, putting her hand on my gear shift. "Now shift with your right hand, and step on the gas with your right foot. Oh, and hold onto the wheel with your left hand." I lurched again. Only this time I practically spun around.

I wasn't happy. I didn't know what direction I was going in. I was stopping and starting and screeching and going in circles and getting very dizzy.

Annabel wasn't happy either. "Left foot, right foot, right hand," she said. "I'll never get it right!" "Sure you will, honey," said Jim, putting his arm around her. "All you need is some practice."

Practice? A *lot* of practice. And better on somebody else. I was a nervous wreck! Oh I liked Annabel all right. I liked her a lot. Except when she was in the driver's seat.

"Tell you what," Jim said after the driving lesson. "After the ball game tonight, we'll take a nice slow ride up to the lake. I hear there's gonna be a full moon."

The lake was one of my favorite spots. It was quiet. I like peace and quiet. And it had pretty scenery, too. Jim and Annabel didn't do much talking. They were busy doing what they called "spooning." I don't know why they called it "spooning." It had *nothing* to do with spoons or food or anything like that. Jim would just sit there with his arm around Annabel, and cuddle her close, and sometimes they'd kiss. Nope. No spoons.

But obviously this "spooning" business must have been very popular, because there was a whole bunch of young people at the University who liked going to the lake to do this, - especially when there was a full moon. I always had plenty of company.

Jim's time at college passed pretty quickly, and

before you knew it, he was a graduate. They made him wear a black gown and a flat hat with a tassel and sit through a whole bunch of speeches. Then they gave him a rolled-up piece of paper and everybody clapped. Doc and Mrs. Wilson were there. So was Annabel. And right after the graduation, Annabel got a new outfit too, only her gown was white and so was her hat, and it was a whole lot prettier than Jim's get-up. Yup. Jim and Annabel got married.

Chapter 4 - BABE RUTH

After the wedding Jim said "Hop in, *Missus* Wilson. We're going to New York City for our honeymoon!"

You want to talk about adventure? Hah! Just go to New York City and you'll have plenty of adventure! Why, the whole place was just overflowing with adventure! I had no idea of where I was or where I was going. It was nothing like Smallville, or even the State U campus.

First off, all the buildings were huge! Higher even than the steeple on the Smallville Church. And there were hundreds of them! And there were bright lights and streetcars. And noise! Oh, Lordy, the noise! Goodbye peace and quiet. Horns were beeping at me left and right, and for no reason at all. I was going along at a nice leisurely clip, minding my own business, taking in all this new scenery, and everybody else was in such a hurry! Cars whizzing by at thirty, maybe thirty-five miles an hour! What's the big rush, I thought? Where's the fire?

And talk about traffic! There were *thousands* of cars on the road, and hardly any horses at all. Nope. It was nothing like Smallville.

Soon after we got settled in New York City, Jim announced that he had a big surprise for Annabel. He held up two tickets. "Ooooh, wow!" exclaimed Annabel, "The Ziegfeld Follies!" That was a fancy-dancy show on Broadway that she had been dying to see. "Nope," said Jim. "We're going to Yankee Stadium! Yessiree," he continued, "We're gonna see the Bambino play! The Sultan of Swat! The Mighty Babe! Babe Ruth!" "Oh," said Annabel in her best try-not-to-be-disappointed voice, since she had her heart set on the Ziegfeld Follies. "Why Annabel, Babe Ruth is the greatest baseball player in the world! We'll be telling our grandchildren about this day," Jim exclaimed. He really loved baseball.

So off we went to Yankee Stadium. I had never heard of this Babe Ruth person, although I came to learn that he was pretty famous. I didn't get to see him play. They stuck me outside of the Stadium with what must've been a *million* other cars. They called it a parking lot - probably because there were a LOT of cars there. Anyway, you should have seen the crowd of people going into that place! And the noise! I could hear the cheering and shouting all the way from where I was parked.

And then, just as I was getting used to all that racket, there was this tre*men*dous roar from inside, and before I knew it, a baseball came flying *right at me*! And it *busted my headlight*! Boy did that hurt! But that's not the end of the story. No sir!

Later, when Jim and Annabel came to get me, everybody was talking about how the great Babe Ruth hit the ball right out of the stadium. Well, when Jim saw my busted headlight and the baseball lying right next to my front wheel, you would think he just hit the jackpot or something! He grabbed the baseball, grabbed Annabel, and ran back into the Stadium. Next thing you know, they were back again with the great Babe Ruth himself - to "inspect the damages." (I still have a slight scar from where I was hit with that baseball.)

Well Babe Ruth was so sorry that he busted my headlight that he gave Jim a *hundred dollars* right then and there. He told Jim to get my headlight fixed, and to take Annabel to dinner and to the Ziegfeld Follies - on him. Then he signed the baseball and gave it to Jim for a souvenir. Now that's what I call a *real good sport*. Jim kept that ball in a glass box on his desk forever.

Chapter 5 - THE FAMILY CAR

After the honeymoon, Jim and Annabel came back to Smallville, which had grown considerably since Jim went to college. They built a new high school that had an athletic field for ball games. And they put up a separate post office. And they built a Washing Machine factory. Can you imagine? A machine to wash your clothes!

Jim got a job with that Washing Machine factory. They said they were looking for bright young college men to be managers. Yessir, Jim was making a name for himself. He had a good job, bought a nice little house for himself and Annabel, and he bought her a washing machine. He also bought one for his mother and for Annabel's mother, too. "I get a good discount," Jim said.

Doc Wilson was always a welcome visitor to our new house. But after a while, he seemed to be coming around more often. Mostly to see

Annabel. One day, Doc put Annabel in his big Pierce-Arrow and took her off to the County Hospital. I was worried sick!

A couple of weeks later, Jim and I brought Annabel home with the *babies*. Yup! Annabel had *twins*! Boy and a girl. This was a whole new experience for me. Doc had a family, of course, but they were pretty much grown. We're talkin' *babies,* here.

"Yoo-hoo, Annabel!" There was a voice at the door, followed by two large suitcases and Annabel's mother. The old battle-axe. Always pushing everybody around, telling 'em what to do. Not my favorite person. "Oh, Mama, I'm so glad you've come to stay," said Annabel. "With these two little bundles of joy, I need all the help I can get!"

Bundles of joy? How about bundles of *noise*? Those two babies had a set of lungs on 'em that matched the entire bleacher section at Yankee Stadium! They weren't too bad when they were asleep, which was a lot, but boy-o-boy, could they make up for it! And then sometimes, I don't know exactly what happened, but there'd be this *awful* smell . . .

But Jim and Annabel were happy about it. I went to work every day with Jim, and on Sunday, if it was nice out, he would take us for picnics at the lake. I always liked the lake, but with the babies and Mama (ugh), it was getting to be a real hassle.

"I don't know why I have to sit in the rumble seat," complained Mama, every time we started out. (You see, I don't have a regular back seat like the modern cars. My back seat was more like where the trunk is. Only I didn't have a trunk.) "I *hate* the rumble seat," she continued, as she started piling more and more paraphernalia into the car.

"But Mama," Jim said kindly, "Where else can you sit? I have to drive. And Annabel and the babies have to sit in the front. And with all the extra stuff we have to take . . ."

Extra stuff? They just about emptied the entire house! In addition to the babies and Mama, we had to take diapers and rattles and bottles and powder and towels and juice and blankets and extra sheets - and the picnic basket. It weighed a *ton*! "Wait!" Jim said, "Let me get my new camera. I want to take a family picture!" So there we were, posing for pictures: Annabel and the babies,

Mama and me - all loaded down with baby-stuff.

"Jim, *JIM*! You're going too fast!" hollered Mama from the rumble seat. "Fifteen miles an hour is a nice safe speed, Mama," Jim said good-naturedly. (Jim was very good-natured.) "Slow down!" insisted Mama, "We've got *babies* in the car!" Hah! As if Jim didn't know.

You probably have guessed that I was never too fond of Mama. I can't understand how a delightful girl like Annabel could have such a grouch for a mother. When Mama wasn't bossing everybody around, she was complaining about something. "I don't like riding back here," Mama grumped. "It's too cramped. Jim, don't you think it's time you got rid of this old heap? Why this jalopy has to be ten years old if it's a minute!"

Old heap? Jalopy? I came to a full stop, hoping Mama would be thrown out of my rumble seat. Get rid of . . .? Why Jim would *never* do a thing like that to me, his old pal. His buddy.

"You have a point, Mama," Jim said, as my heart was about to break. "I love this car, but T really is too small for us now. A wife, two babies and a mother-in-law," he sighed, "I hate to say it, but I'll have to get a bigger car. And," he added happily, "since I just got a nice raise at the Washing Machine factory, I suppose I can afford it."

What about me? What'll I do? Where will I go?

Annabel must have read my mind. "What will you do with T?" she asked. "Sell 'im, I guess. If anybody wants a nine year old car," Jim answered. "How about Fred Mahoney at the service station?" Annabel suggested. "He bought the general store last year, and his kids are getting big. He could probably use T for making deliveries."

Well that wouldn't be so bad, I thought. I liked Fred Mahoney. He always took good care of me. I could be useful. I knew my way all around town so I would never get lost. And I knew just about all of Fred's customers. I liked Fred's kids, too - especially Joe. He reminded me a lot of Jim, when he was younger. And it wouldn't be so noisy.

Chapter 6 - I AM A MAHONEY

When Fred was approached by Jim, he said "Sure I'd be interested in your old Model-T Ford. The store's been doing a fair business, and the boys could drive it to make deliveries. How much do you want?" "Three hundred dollars," said Jim. "Fair 'nuf," said Fred. "It's a deal."

So Jim and I parted company, but we were still best friends. I went to live with the Mahoneys, and Jim bought a big new spiffy Buick. Sometimes I would see Jim driving with Annabel and the babies. And Mama. I'd beep at him, and he'd beep back and wave! It wasn't bad at all.

The Mahoneys were good people. Fred Junior and Tim helped out in the store after school, and Joe used to drive me on deliveries. In those days you didn't need a driver's license. All you needed was to know how to drive.

Sometimes Joe would drive me across town

with a bag of groceries for old Mrs. Murphy. He'd bring the bag inside and help her put everything away because she limped and walked with a cane. Mrs. Murphy would always give Joe a nickel for his efforts, and tell him to buy a soda-pop.

Not long after I became a Mahoney, something happened to Smallville. For one thing, the Washing Machine factory where my old pal Jim worked? They closed up. They said times were hard and people couldn't afford washing machines. A lot of folks were moving out of town, including Jim and Annabel and the babies. And Mama. He packed up the new Buick and moved to the City. There was more work there.

I was desolate. Fred Mahoney was barely getting by. Times were really bad. People weren't coming into the store very often, let alone having their cars fixed or getting gas. There was no place to go and no money to get there if there was, so why get gas?

Oh, there was a dance every so often at the Elks, and of course there was always the big Fourth of July parade and picnic. Fred and his family would decorate me with red-white-and-blue crepe paper and American flags, and we'd go up to the lake. That was always fun - if it didn't rain. The high school band played a few songs and the Mayor made a nice speech, and once in a while our Congressman would show up. Fred would sell a lot of hot dogs and soda-pop then.

But aside from special events like the high school graduation, about the only excitement around Smallville was the weekly checkers match at the general store. Homer Schmidlapp was probably the best checkers player in town, and he took on all comers.

One time Edna Mae Willoughby's nephew Floyd was visiting from out of state, and decided to challenge Homer. Boyoboy what a turnout that night! Homer was excited about having some "new blood" as he called it. He beat just about everybody else in the county. People were torn between wanting Homer to win for "our town" and getting a little tired of Homer winning all the time.

Homer lost. Edna Mae Willoughby's nephew Floyd was a good checkers player, too - particularly for an eleven-year-old. But Homer was a good sport and bought the kid a soda-pop to show there were no hard feelings. Fred sold a *lot* of soda-pop that night.

Those years were a sorry time. I sat outside Fred's general store and garage for the most part. I hardly got driven at all. Cost of gas, they said. Seventeen cents a gallon! Joe made deliveries on his bicycle. "Muscle power doesn't cost anything," Fred said.

Chapter 7 - I AM STOLEN

But once there was some *real* excitement. I mean real *in-the-newspapers* excitement! A couple of strangers hiked into town. They seemed to be just young kids, but there was something about them I didn't care for.

"Tough luck about our car breaking down outside," said the bigger kid, whose name, I came to find out, was Frank. "What are we gonna do, Frank?" asked the smaller one, which was how I learned that the big kid was named Frank. "There's a price on our heads after the last robbery! We're wanted in three counties! We gotta get outa here fast!" O boy, I thought. This is trouble.

"Don't worry, little sister," said Frank, patting his companion on the head. "I'll think of something." He turned around. I tried very hard to look invisible, but no luck. "Hey, here's an old car right here," he said, looking straight at me. "Aaaah, this old heap won't get us anywhere.

Gotta be fifteen years old," said "little sister." "It'll get us further than walkin'," Frank said, "and a whole lot faster. You get it cranked up, and I'll see what I can get inside."

Frank put a bandanna over his face and went into the general store. I wanted to beep my horn and warn Fred, but . . . Meanwhile, "little sister" was cranking and cranking. I wasn't budging, of course. I knew what was happening. I wasn't going to co-operate.

"C'mon you old bucket of bolts! C'mon, c'mon," said the girl, cranking as hard as she could, which was surprisingly strong for a girl her size. I still wouldn't move - especially when I heard the voices inside the store.

Fred Mahoney must have been working behind the counter and didn't see the bandanna over Frank's face, because he greeted him pleasantly enough. "How-do, son. What can I get for you?" Fred was always nice to passing strangers. They usually bought a soda-pop when they asked for directions or gas. "You can give me all that cash in the drawer," said a muffled voice. Fred turned and saw Frank with the bandanna. And a *gun* in his hand!

Fred stayed calm. One thing about Fred, he didn't get excited much. Besides, the boy didn't look any older than Tim or Fred Junior. "Now son," said Fred, "You don't want to do a dumb thing like that. If you're broke and hungry, I'd be glad to..." Frank's voice was rough. "I said gimme the cash and be quick about it! Ain't got time to chat . . ." "OK, OK," said Fred, trying to keep cool. "Just put the gun down. Don't shoot."

Shoot??? Gun??? There was *NO WAY* I was going to start, even though the girl put some gas in my tank and was cranking away. Fred was in trouble and I had to help. Then the girl added injury to all the insults, and kicked me hard in a couple of places. "You're gonna start up you miserable old crate, or my name ain't Jessie James!"

I started shaking. I heard of Jessie James and her brother Frank before. Not only did I start, but my engine was really racing.

Frank moved closer to the door. "Twelve bucks?" he complained. "That ain't much." "We're poor people, too. That's all I got," Fred said, still trying to stay calm. "Too bad," said Frank. Then there was a pistol shot!! Frank ran out, still wearing the bandanna, hopped on my running board, and Jessie drove away as fast as I could go. As a matter of fact, it was faster than I'd ever gone before.

Fred wrapped his wounded arm in a towel and hollered for help. The police chief came right away and deputized nearly half the town! There must have been a dozen cars chasing us. Chasing and *shooting* at us! And blowing whistles and sirens! I desperately wanted to stop, but Jessie's foot had pressed my gas pedal to the floor, and there was no way I *could* stop. I thought about crashing into something, but I have to say that Jessie James was one heckuva good driver - a lot better than Annabel ever was!

Every time the sheriff gained on us, Jessie would make a sharp turn, or drive off the road and through a field. Meanwhile Frank kept shooting his gun and yelling at Jessie to go faster. We got about ten miles out of town, when all of a sudden, a bunch of cars were blocking our way! The police chief had called the County Sheriff and they had all the roads blocked. I breathed a sigh of relief. At last! But then Jessie made a sharp curve around the police cars and we continued. Or at least we continued a few hundred feet. Jessie didn't know about the ditch on the side of the road.

Down we went, and over the rocks. Jessie was screaming and Frank was hollering a few words I never heard before, but they didn't sound too polite. Anyway, I came to a full stop, nose-to-nose with a big pine tree. The police chief and all the deputies and the Sheriff's officers charged down the hill after us. They took Frank's gun away, and made Frank and Jessie James climb out of the ditch with their hands up. Then they put handcuffs on them and carted them off to jail.

That was quite a day. I was banged up pretty badly, but thank goodness Fred Mahoney only had a slight wound, and Doc Wilson fixed him right up. They needed two horses plus Bud Johnson's tractor to haul *me* out of the ditch.

It was in all the papers. Even in papers hundreds of miles away. "James Gang Arrested in Smallville." Hah! But one good thing came of it. It put Smallville on the map, at least for a little while. Everybody came. Reporters, photographers, radio people - even tourists. Everybody wanted to see where they caught Frank and Jessie James - and, ahem, to see me. The famous getaway car. And when people come, they bring money.

The store business picked up for a few months. Fred sold a lot of soda-pop. He fixed me up, too. Good as new, almost. I have a few more scars, and you don't have to look that close, either.

But it didn't take long for the novelty to wear off. A few months of being a celebrity, and poof! Right back to the same old stuff. People were calling it a depression. The hard times just wouldn't go away. And just about the time I figured my life was going to be one long rut, I met her.

T

Chapter 8 - GLORIA

I was sitting outside Fred's store and garage one August day, when the most beautiful car I had ever seen pulled up next to me. It was a big car. New and long and sleek. And white. I had never seen a white car before. Matter of fact, I never saw a car in any other color but black, except for the fire engine. And not only was the car white, but when I peeked inside, the seats and the wheel were white, too. And covered with some kind of fur!

I cleared my throat, and in the most respectful voice I could muster, I said, "How-do, ma'am," just like I heard Fred Mahoney say so many times in the store. "I've never seen you around before. New in town?" I tried being casual, but my engine was racing. "Just passin' through," came the softest voice I had ever heard.

I was unable to control my admiration. "You're beautiful," I blurted out. "I hope you don't mind my saying so, but you're the most beautiful car

I've ever seen! My name is T. I'm a Model-T Ford." "Mah name is Gloria. Ah'm a Cadillac," she said. A Cadillac! Wow! I had heard of Cadillacs before. Very classy. *Ver-ry* expensive. So in my best non-chalant attitude, I said, "Oh. This is the first time I've ever seen a Cadillac. I mean, up close." I peeked through the window again. "Is that real fur?"

"Fur?" Gloria replied haughtily. "This happens to be genuine imitation *ermine*." I was duly impressed. "Oh," I said, since I didn't know what else to say. "What brings you to Smallville?"

"We're on our way back to Hollywood, California," Gloria announced. "Mah ownah is Miss Daphne Ritzswanky, the famous European movie stah." Boy-o-boy-o-BOY-o-boy!! I had been to the movies a few times with Jim and Annabel. I even went once with Joe Mahoney and a girl he knew from high school. But that was a long time ago. I could hardly believe that a famous movie actress was right here in Smallville and I was having a conversation with her *magnificent* car!

"Mah ownah, Miss Daphne Ritzswanky, the famous European movie stah, stopped heah to freshen up, have lunch, and, ahem, get gas for me," Gloria continued. "Ah take twelve gallons."

"Twelve gallons," I said as my headlights opened wide. "That'll make *my* owner real happy. Fred Mahoney hardly sells twelve gallons in a week, let alone to one car. One very beautiful car."

Gloria checked her rear view mirror and adjusted her big headlights. "Do you really think so?" she asked coyly. "Oh indeed I do," I said. "Do you think maybe you could talk your owner into getting you a tune up and an oil change, too? I mean, you'd be able to stay a little longer, and it would make my owner real happy. And I'd be glad to show you the sights. We've got a movie house, the diner, the high school athletic field and the closed-up Washing Machine factory. Lots of neat stuff," I said, adding, "And a real nice lake." My head swam with visions of being alone with Gloria. At the lake.

Gloria coughed slightly. "Well ah suppose ah have been feelin' a bit run down lately," she said. "And it *is* a long *long* way to Hollywood, California . . ."

I was carried away. "And if Miss Daphne Ritzswanky, the famous European movie star, stays around for a while, I'm sure the whole *town* will turn out to give her a big welcome!" I promised.

Well as luck would have it, it just so happened that Daphne Ritzswanky was a movie star all right, but no more European than Babe Ruth - or Fred Mahoney, for that matter. Turns out she was just plain Lottie Glotz from Midville, and the Hollywood studios made up that European stuff along with her new name. It also turns out that the Glotzes were related to the Plodniks, who lived across the street from the Klunk's Uncle Angus, who was second cousin to Fred Mahoney's brother-in-law. Well, that made Lottie Glotz, pardon me, Miss Daphne Ritzswanky, practically *family* in Smallville. She stayed a week.

"It's nice how the town turned out to welcome mah ownah, Miss Daphne Ritzswanky, the famous European movie stah," said Gloria as we were driving up to the lake. (Actually, the town came out to welcome Lottie Glotz from Midville, but that's another story.) "You know," I began, feeling a bit expansive, "I'm not just another hick car from the country. I was stolen once - by the famous James gang. Frank and his sister Jessie. And I've been to New York City, too. And to Yankee Stadium, where I met the great Babe Ruth. Personally."

Gloria didn't seem impressed with my

adventures. She was all gussied up for her trip to Hollywood, California. "Is this the lake you were telling me about?" she asked, as we parked under a couple of tall elm trees. "Yup," I said, "nice isn't it? Cool breeze, full Harvest moon . . ." "Careful, not too close," said Gloria. "Ah've just been washed, waxed, had mah oil changed, mah tires ro-tated and took, ahem, twelve-point-three gallons."

I was in awe. Boy-o-boy! "Fred Mahoney really did a job on you," I exclaimed in admiration. She really did look beautiful. "Best beauty treatment Ah've evah had," she said, checking her rear view mirror. "Your ownah really knows how to treat a lady." Needless to say, I was on my very best Sunday behavior.

"Well, T," Gloria said finally, "It's been real nice knowin' you. You've been a perfect gentleman. If you evah get to Hollywood, California, you be sure to come on up and see me sometime." And she drove away and out of my life.

I could barely sputter a goodbye. Sigh. I'll say this, though - I never see a harvest moon without thinking of Gloria. I wonder whatever became of her. I know about Daphne Ritzswanky, alias Lottie Glotz. She made a pile of money in

Hollywood, retired, died at the ripe old age of ninety-one and left a fortune to her cat.

But back to my story. I spent a lot of years with Fred Mahoney and his family. Doc Wilson would stop in every so often to fill up his Pierce Arrow, so I got to find out that my pals Jim and Annabel were doing pretty well in the City, hard times notwithstanding. The twins were fine and getting big, and they had two more kids after that.

But times were changing again. Seems there was a War on, and Smallville was right smack in the middle of activity.

T

Chapter 9 - ON THE HOMEFRONT

Those war years were tough. The Depression years were tough for sure, but this was a different kind of tough. People were worried a lot and listened to the radio all the time. But they were more cheerful for the most part, and strange as it may seem, there was more money for soda-pop, which was one of the few things that wasn't rationed.

A lot of Smallville boys went off to War, including all three of Fred Mahoney's sons. Fred was proud of them, but he worried and he'd stand at the door waiting for the mailman every day.

I got a new owner, sort of. Peggy Mahoney. Can you believe it? Peggy was twenty years old and a very pretty young lady. Seems like yesterday when she was born!

Anyway, one of the reasons there was more money for soda-pop was because of the Old

Washing Machine factory. The government said it would be a dandy place to make spare airplane parts, which was very important to the war effort, so lots of people were put to work, including Peggy.

Peggy got a job as a Class I Mechanic, and she was very good at it. She learned a lot hanging around her father's garage. She drove the carpool with her girlfriends Sue and Sally, since they were only allowed to buy three gallons of gasoline a week. I was *always* hungry.

"Hi, Peg," said Sally, getting in one morning at eight o'clock. "Congratulations on being Employee of the Week!" "Thanks," Peg replied. "I worked hard for it, and that five dollar bonus will come in real handy!" "I'll bet," said Sally. "By the way, did you hear from Sam?" "Yup," grinned Peggy. "He's fine and he misses me." They drove over to pick up Sue.

"Hi," Sue said, getting into my rumble seat. "Have you heard from Joe lately? I haven't gotten a letter in a long time." Sue was Joe's special girl. They took me to the lake a few times before the War. "Not since last month when he said they were shipping out," said Peggy. "I'm scared," said Sue. "My dad said not to worry. He said it's hard to handle mail on a ship," replied Peggy. "We'll probably get a dozen letters all at once." That cheered Sue a bit.

"Peg! Look at the time! We'd better step on it before Old Lady MacKenzie has a conniption!" said Sally. "She's such a fuss-pot about the time clock." I went a little faster. After all, I didn't want the girls to be late. I heard stories about Miss MacKenzie, and while I never met her personally, it sounded to me that she was a lot like Annabel's mother. The old battle-axe.

"Let's get to work *on time,* ladies," said Peggy, imitating Miss MacKenzie, "Don't you know there's a war on?" Of course we knew there was a War on. Fred Mahoney waited for the mail every morning, and every evening he'd listen to the news on the radio and read the newspapers. Everyone else in town was doing the same thing.

Peggy and her girlfriends were terrific! They put on coveralls and went out to do the men's jobs, and did a mighty fine job of it. But me? Oh, I got driven back and forth to the factory and around town some. But three gallons of gas a week doesn't exactly encourage sight-seeing.

But then again, I was getting on in years, and I

figured I'd probably retire. The new models they came out with after the War had features I never even dreamed about! They didn't need cranks. Just turn a key and poof! Starts right up! And they had wide rubber tires and big roomy seats - even in the back. And they had trunks for storage. No more rumble seats. They had easy roll-up-and-down windows, and some cars - hah! Some even had a *radio* so you could listen to Bing Crosby sing while you were driving. Can you believe it? A *radio* in the car? And they could whiz by at fifty or even sixty miles an hour! What's the big hurry?

My first owner, Doc Wilson? He passed away during the War years. But he was around seventy-five, and had a fine, full life. I learned about my old pals Jim and Annabel when they came for Doc's funeral. Jim had a real good job in the City. The company made all sorts of fancy-dancy electrical stuff, and Jim was a big-shot manager. I always said that boy was smart! I think he said the company was called G-something. G-B, G-E. Whatever. He didn't go off to war. He was a few years over age, and with the four kids and his important job, they said he was more valuable here.

Peggy Mahoney's boyfriend Sam was promoted for bravery. He came home a sergeant, and they got married. Fred Mahoney's oldest boy, Fred Junior? They made him a Captain. And Tim got three medals. But Joe didn't come home. His ship was torpedoed somewhere in the Pacific. It was a sad, sad day when the telegram came.

But this is *my* story. So, like I said, I figured I'd retire, and I sort of did for a while. I sat outside Fred Mahoney's garage with a pot of geraniums on my hood, and a sign saying "For Sale to a Good Owner. Cheap."

Fred Mahoney was thinking about retiring too. He said his rheumatism was getting pesky and the boys were doing a fine job with the store. Fine job, did I say? They were doing a *super* job! Fred Junior and Tim put up a big new sign that said "Mahoney & Sons Supermarket." They put in a lot more stock, added a parking lot, since just about everybody had a car now, and they were even thinking about putting up another store across town. They bought a station wagon for deliveries.

Yup, times were changing again. Every week, Fred would check me out and drive me over to Peggy and Sam's. But for the most part, I just sat with the geraniums. It wasn't bad. It was nice and quiet. And it smelled good.

Then one day Spike Mulligan showed up.

FOR
SALE
TO GOOD
OWNER
CHEAP
T

Chapter 10 - THE BREAKNECK BUGGY

I never met anybody who looked like Spike Mulligan before. For one thing, he wore sunglasses - and the sun wasn't shining. He was dressed all in black, from his hat to his boots. And he wore a black leather jacket with big studs in it, and on the back it had a skull and crossbones. And he was smoking a cigarette. This was not comforting.

"Hey," he said, snapping his fingers. Fred Mahoney looked up. Fred was not used to being snapped at. "You talkin' to me?" he asked calmly. "Nah, your grandmother," said Spike. Spike was obviously not inclined to good manners. "What can I do for you?" Fred said in a not-too-happy voice. Fred was used to people talking with respect.

"Heard you got an old car for sale. Cheap." Spike was staring at me and my sign. I was petrified. "It's just an old car. Not your style," said Fred, trying to be discouraging. Atta boy, Fred, I thought. You'll save me! "I'm lookin' for an old junker," said Spike. "Oh?" said Fred. "Yeah," said Spike. "This it?" He handed my geraniums to Fred and started to check me out. "That's it," said Fred, who was about as happy as I was. "It's a real old Model-T Ford. Gotta be thirty years old if it's a day."

Spike tried cranking me up, and of course I wouldn't budge. He looked under my hood and I coughed and sputtered as loud as I could. "Still run?" asked Spike after I conked out on him three times in a row. "Always did for me," Fred said, "but, heh, heh, I wouldn't plan on goin' real far." Fred was definitely trying to be discouraging. "Think it could make it around a two-mile track?" asked Spike, checking my wheels.

"Track?" asked Fred suspiciously. "Yeah," said Spike in a pleasanter voice. "My buddies and I like to race these old jalopies. Sometimes we even take 'em to the County Fair. People'll pay good money to see us bang up these old crates."

Bang up these old crates??? This was *NOT* what I had in mind for my golden years. If I had knees, I'd have been on them. Fred! Do something!! We've been through so much together!

"Well," said Fred, "Ol' T has been part of the family for years. I really couldn't let him go . . ." "How's three hundred dollars? Cash." Spike reached for his wallet. Fred was astonished. That was about five times more than he expected.

"Three hundred, huh?" Fred nodded slowly, and patted my roof. "That's a good offer. And I could use the money to put in those frozen foods the boys keep talking about. It's a deal. He's yours." Fred took the money, gave me a wistful sigh, and all of a sudden I belonged to Spike Mulligan.

"Well, Pal," Spike said, finally getting me to start, "we'll get you fixed up as one of the gang. We're gonna be spending a lot of time together."

Gang? I wasn't meant for gangs. I was meant for geraniums. This was not a high point in my life. OK, so maybe I was a little smug after all my years with the Wilsons and the Mahoneys. Spike Mulligan and his pals were hot-rodders, and they dragged me to hot-rod rodeos and just about wore me out.

"You really think you can race this piece of junk?" asked Tank. Tank was Spike's best pal, and when you looked at him, you understood why people called him Tank. He was the biggest guy I ever saw. "Sure I can!" Spike said with enthusiasm, and he pulled out a long list. "Of course I'll have to gut the insides. Get a completely new transmission. Get rid of the old engine, put in a super-charged V-8 . . . oughta be able to get up to fifty, maybe sixty miles an hour."

Fifty or sixty . . .? Just to ride in circles? I felt faint at the thought.

"Give 'im some new shocks, brakes, new wide-rimmed tires, a fancy paint job . . ." Spike ran down the list. "How about Outrageous Orange?" suggested Spike's girlfriend Angie. "He'll really stand out in the crowd!" "Yeah, Ang," said Spike. Orange. Good idea. Hah! This baby'll be the envy of the Demolition Derby!"

Dem-o-li-tion Derby? I want my geraniums!

"Y'know, Spike, three hundred bucks is a lot! Plus all the fixin' up. I sure hope you know what you're doin'," said Tank. "It is a lot," agreed Spike, "But the chassis on this bucket is solid as a rock. If I can win two or three races and then junk it for parts, I oughta make out fine. What'll I call it? I need something catchy."

"How about the Breakneck Buggy?" suggested

Angie. "Great name! The Breakneck Buggy. I'll paint the name across the side in big black letters. 'Breakneck Buggy'!" Spike grinned, but he still wasn't my cup of tea. I didn't like the name either, but I didn't have any say in the matter.

Do you have any idea what they do at these Demolotion Derbies? They race old cars around a track, they crash into each other on purpose, and the last one left standing - or moving - is the winner. This is supposed to be great fun.

Spike Mulligan must have been a very good hot-rod driver. He got five, yes *five* races out of me before I caved in. I got revved and raced and banged and busted. I don't think there was any part of me that wasn't completely black and blue under all that orange paint. And I never did get used to the noise of all that crashing around. But I won most of my races. Mister Henry Ford built us pretty tough, I guess. I was a survivor. We went to the State Fair and Spike won twenty-five hundred dollars in prize money. We even had our picture in the paper. "Spike Mulligan and his Breakneck Buggy."

Oh, Spike wasn't all that bad, I suppose. Each time we raced, he fixed me right up. He didn't skimp. I had the best parts he could find. And he spent a lot of time with me, so we learned to appreciate each other.

Then Spike decided that we were both too old for that kind of punishment, so he opened a truck-stop out on the highway and he sent me off to the "Old Car Home." The junkyard. Spike sold off the fancy-dancy engine and brakes and tires and just about everything of value. He got around three hundred dollars for it, if I remember correctly. Then he carted me off. Good-bye.

362
T

Chapter 11 - THE OLD CAR HOME

So there I was just an empty shell. Couldn't start, couldn't go anywhere. I couldn't do anything except pass the time of day with the other junk.

"Hey, T, didja hear the news?" asked Stu one day, many years after I was brought to the Old Car Home. "News? What kind of news is there in a junkyard?" "We're getting another clunker in here. Ed just saw a guy pull in with an old Volkswagen." "A Volkswagen?" I repeated, "I thought those cars *never* wore out!" "You know as well as I do that you don't have to be old to be here. Just obsolete," said Stu.

Stu was right. He was an old Studebaker, and they stopped making them long about the time I started my racing career. "Yup," continued Stu, "When they stopped making us Studebakers, nobody could get parts. And shucks, Ed, you were only six or seven when you got scrapped." "Sad but true," said Ed. "Nobody wanted Edsels.

We were orphans from birth."

"I wonder what the new car will be like," I mused. It had been such a long time since we had a new face in the Old Car Home. It would be nice to have someone else to talk to, much as I liked Stu and Ed. "Now T," started Ed, "I hope you're not gonna bore the new car to death with your old stories." "May be old stories to you," I defended, "but to a new car . . ." Stu wouldn't let me finish. "Lissen," he said, "If I hear about Babe Ruth one more time . . ." "Or the tall tale about Frank and Jessie James," Ed said cutting him off. "But those are *true* stories," I protested. "Yeah, yeah," they said.

We needed a new face. We were starting to get on each others' nerves.

"Ja, shentelmen," came a distinctively feminine voice, "dis iss vere I go. Der last shtop." The new Volkswagen was a lady! And about time! "Fellas, your manners," I reminded my pals, as we greeted her. "Welcome to the Old Car Home, Miss Volkswagen," said Stu. "I'm Stu, a 1945 Studebaker. They don't make 'em like me anymore!" "And I'm Ed," said the Edsel. "A 1955 genuine Edsel. They *never* made 'em like me!" We all laughed. Ed continued, "And this here is my grandfather, ha ha. This is T, an old Model-T Ford from when? 1920? 1921?" "Hard to remember," I said, "It was a long time ago."

"Call me Fraulein," said the Volkswagen. "Dat's vat my owners called me. I'm from nineteen-sixty-vun." "All those years and you still have an accent?" Ed asked. "Ve didn't talk much," said Fraulein. "Dey played loud radio, ja?" "I still can't believe it," I said, "A radio in a car!"

"So," Fraulein continued, "vat does effrebody do here?" "We sit," said Stu. "None of us have engines." Ed added, "I'm missing wheels, my transmission and the back door." "And I'm missing hmmpf. I'm missing everything," I said, "except my memories. Yes ma'am, I've got some wonderful memories . . ."

Stu and Ed cut me off with a blunt, "Enough. Let's show Fraulein some of the sights." They pointed to some of the old washing machines and stand-up radios that were lying around nearby.

"I think it's somewhere around here, Jean," I heard a distinctly human voice say. My ears perked up. There was something in that voice that was vaguely familiar. "But there's so much junk, how are you *ever* going to find it?" That was definitely a female voice. I looked around as best I could, and saw a man and a woman dressed in some fancy-dancy jogging suits that everybody likes now.

"I don't know," said the man. "Instinct maybe. Besides, I have an old photo grandpa took when Dad was a baby." He came a little closer to where we were, and started poking around. We weren't easy to find, especially since we were all bunched up together, with about three dozen old tires piled around us. "It's gotta be here someplace," the man insisted, "and I've always wanted to fix up a really vintage car. My old '65 Mustang is fun, but I want something exotic." The woman didn't sound quite as enthusiastic. "Grown up boys, same old toys," she said. The man continued, "And I remember grandpa telling me all those old stories about T, and how they went to Yankee Stadium . . ." He started poking through a long row of ancient washing machines.

Yankee Stadium? What about Yankee Stadium? I was suddenly alert. The cars here never even heard of Yankee Stadium. I was listening intently. "Yup," the man continued, "Grandpa must have told me that story a hundred times about the busted headlight and how he met Babe Ruth."

"Listen up, you guys," I nudged Stu and Ed. "You thought my stories about Babe Ruth were just an old car's ramblings!"

"And you know that old baseball of his that Babe Ruth signed?" the man went on, "I bet it's worth a bundle!"

Babe Ruth? THE Babe Ruth? My old pal the Bambino? Over here, fella! I can tell you a few things about Babe Ruth!

The man was still working his way through the washing machines, getting very close to my pal Ed. "Nope," he said, "This is an old Edsel. Defunct. Y'know, Jean, this would be good for the Antique Car Show. I'll have to tell some of the guys about this place. I bet they could get the Edsel for peanuts."

"Jeff, even if you found an old Model-T, how could you be sure it was the same one your grandpa had?" asked Jean, examining a washing machine that had been junked long before World War II. "And how come there are so many washing machines here?"

"They had a washing machine factory around here a zillion years ago," said Jeff. "Grandpa got his first job there after he graduated from the university." Jeff was coming closer to me and I could just about get a look at him. "It's gotta be the Model-T I'm looking for," he continued. "Grandpa sold it to a guy named Fred Mahoney, and I checked back at Mahoney's Supermarket. The old guy remembered it from when he was a kid. Said his name was Tim. They sold it after the war."

Jean stopped climbing through the pile of old washing machines and came closer to where Jeff stood. "He's the one that knows your grandfather, right?" "Yup," said Jeff. "Remind me to tell Mom so she can invite him to Grandpa's ninetieth birthday party. That should be a hoot!"

They were close to where I was buried now, and when I took a good look, I could hardly contain myself. Why Jeff looked so much like my old pal Jim Wilson it was incredible! I wiped a tear from my eye.

Hey guys, here I am! It's me! It's me!

Jeff was now poking around near my buddy Stu. "Stu," I said, "move over so this guy can find me! We're family! Did you hear what he said about Babe Ruth?" But poor Stu, with no transmission, couldn't budge.

"Anyway," continued Jeff, "Tim Mahoney sent me to that old geezer Elwood Mulligan out on the highway. He showed me all those old pictures and clippings of his hot-rod days forty years ago. I couldn't shut the old guy up. Said nobody wants to talk about the good old days anymore."

I do! I want to talk about all those things! My goodness, I can't get over the resemblance! And the girl reminds me a lot of Annabel. I like them already.

Jeff was getting awfully close. "And the Mulligan guy said he stripped the car for parts and junked him here forty years ago! There aren't any other Model-T's in the whole area." "But even if you find it, it'll be all rusted and banged up," Jean said. She was right. I was a mess. Definitely not ready for a family reunion.

"I don't care, Jean" Jeff insisted. "All I need is the shell. I can fix everything else. And if I can't, I'll find somebody who can. Hah! Won't *that* impress some of those dudes at the Club. Why Charlie McCord has been absolutely unbearable since he got that old white Cadillac. Said it used to belong to a movie star! Hmmmpf!"

White Cadillac? Movie star? Nah, couldn't be.

"Y'know, Jean," Jeff went on, "Mr. Mulligan said he painted the car a bright orange. Maybe we should be looking for something orange!"

Over here, boy, over here! C'mon guys, help me up! I have no engine!

My pals had no engines either. Jeff was so close now I could practically touch him.

"Look Jean, help me with this. I see a patch of orange right here - wedged between the Edsel and the Studebaker," Jeff cried. "Hey, look at this old Volkswagen," Jean said pointing to Fraulein. "My dad had one of those when I was a kid." "This is it Jean! I'm sure of it. Look at where the wheels would be - if it had wheels!"

It's me! It's me! I could have hugged him!

"How can you be sure?" asked Jean skeptically. "I just know it," said Jeff. "Gut maybe, but it's like this car is talking to me!"

Of COURSE I'm talking to you, son! My goodness how he looks like his grandpa.

"I've gotta have it, Jean!" Jeff insisted as he pulled away some of the old tires that were surrounding me. "Give the junkman three hundred bucks and see if he'll help me haul this car out of here." "Three *hundred*?" exclaimed Jean. I was amazed myself. That was a lot of money. "That's what Grandpa got from Fred Mahoney. Figured it's worth that much to me, too. Besides, when I get finished with old T, he'll be worth a hundred times that amount!"

The junkman was thrilled with three hundred dollars. He and Jeff unwedged me from the Old Car Home, hooked me to the back of Jeff's nifty van, and took me to my new home.

"Hey, T, tell him about *us*," said Ed as we were leaving. "We'd love to find a new home, too!" I promised to do my best.

Chapter 12 - "Q"

After I left Stu said, "I can't believe that after all those years T finally got adopted. I'm gonna miss that old goat and all his stories." "I can't believe there really was a Babe Ruth person and that he was actually telling the truth!" said Ed, in amazement.

"I know sometink about dose Antique Car Shows," said Fraulein. "Really?" asked Stu and Ed, "What are they like?" "Ach," the Volkswagen began, "Dey are vunderful. Sometimes dey go to der Fair or ride in parades. Nice und slow. Vit dignity. Und effrybody turns to look. Dere owners paint und polish dem und put in new glass und engines. Der verks! Costs a fortune! Und dey keep 'em in a garage - not out in der rain und snow. Nice und varm. Dey get vunderful care. Und you know vat else?"

"Vat?" asked Stu and Ed, getting carried away by Fraulein's description. "Dey have special license plates, vit a "Q" on dem, so dat effrybody knows it's a special car!" "Oh I'd like to be one of those cars," said Stu. "Me too," sighed Ed. "Me tree," said Fraulein.

So every story should have a happy ending and this one is no exception. I don't think anyone could be happier than I was. Jeff Wilson fixed me up like I've never been fixed before. You think Spike Mulligan did a job on me? Hah! That was nothing! Jeff put in all new parts and fixed me up good as new. Better! My new insides took *years* off my age, and I felt as sprightly as, well . . . as a Thunderbird!

His grandpa Jim couldn't believe he really found me! We recognized each other at once, but that's how it always is with old pals. Jim even said he could still see the scar from where I got hit with Babe Ruth's baseball . . . but I think old Jim's eyesight may be playing a few tricks on him.

Jeff told his friends at the Club about Stu and Ed and Fraulein, and those guys swarmed around the Smallville junkyard like bees in a field of daisies. I run into them fairly often at shows and they just grin from fender to fender. None of us could have imagined that this would happen to us so late in our careers.

Old Spike Mulligan came to see me once at the Fair. He couldn't believe it was really me, till Jeff showed him an old broken piece of orange fender and a whole bunch of "before" pictures. "Before" he fixed me up, that is. But then again, Spike had changed over the years, too. He wore regular glasses now, and stopped smoking.

Best of all, I get a chance to make lots of new friends, and occasionally run into an old one, like last month . . .

"Gloria?" I couldn't believe my eyes! "Gloria? Is that you?" There was a big, beautiful white Cadillac looking so much like the one I remembered so long ago. "Oh mah," said the Cadillac, flashing her big shiny headlights, "Ah haven't been called 'Gloria' in fifty years." My engine raced.

"But it *is* you! You *are* Gloria, aren't you? A Cadillac. You used to be owned by . . ." "Miss Daphne Ritzswanky, the famous European movie stah," Gloria said proudly, trying to summon up her own long-forgotten memories. "Remember me?" I asked hopefully, "I'm T, the Model-T Ford! We met in Smallville years and years ago. We went to the lake . . . and spooned . . ."I prayed that she would remember.

Gloria turned and seemed very impressed by the job Jeff Wilson did on me. "Oh, T," she said admiringly, "Ah do remember you. You were always such a fine gentleman."

She flashed her headlights again and I moved up to escort her at the head of the parade. "And you're still the most beautiful car I've ever seen," I said gallantly, riding alongside. "Did I ever tell you about the time I went to Yankee Stadium and met the great Babe Ruth?"

THE END

Printed in the United States
61633LVS00001B/199-294

9 780978 515836